BIG-TIME BUSINESS

CASHING IN?
THE BANKING INDUSTRY

Sarah Levete

W
FRANKLIN WATTS
LONDON • SYDNEY

First published 2015 by Franklin Watts
338 Euston Road
London NW1 3BH

Franklin Watts Australia
Level 17/207 Kent Street
Sydney, NSW 2000

Produced by Calcium

A CIP catalogue record for this book is available from
the British Library.

ISBN 978 1 4451 3914 2

Dewey classification: 332.1

Printed in China

Franklin Watts is a division of Hachette Children's Books,
an Hachette UK company
www.hachette.co.uk

Acknowledgements:
The publisher would like to thank the following for permission to reproduce
photographs: Cover: Shutterstock: Kayros Studio l, Yakobchuk Vasyl c, Ash Design
background. Inside: Bank of England: 9t; Dreamstime: Bowie15 24, Tomasz Bidermann
45, Alex Gunningham 38bl; Istockphoto: Matthias Haas 28–29, Josh Laverty 41t,
Skip ODonnell 30bl, Patrick Poendl 44–45, Trevor Smith 40bl; Library of Congress:
33t; RMN: R. G. Ojéda 6–7; Shutterstock: 17t, 360b 39b, Africa924 27t, Andy Dean
Photography 35t, Yuri Arcurs 11b, Bikeriderlondon 16b, Gerry Boughan 43t, Ben Bryant
22r, Rachelle Burnside 8tr, Chen WS 23, Cloki 15tr, P Cruciatti 1cl, Discpicture 37,
Forestpath 20b, Angelo Giampiccolo 25t, Gil C 13, Richard Griffin 11tr, Haveseen 3cr,
Magicinfoto 28bl, McIek 12bl, Media Bakery13 40br, Monkey Business Images 19t, R
Nagy 10, Parinyabinsuk 18b, Ragnarock 1cr, 4b, Alexander Raths 34br, Rido 14b, Sean
Pavone Photo 30–31, Galushko Sergey 6br, SVLuma 4bl, Pavel Svoboda 42b, Artur
Synenko 6bc, Liviu Toader 15bl, Wavebreakmedia 5, Lisa F. Young 21c, Serg Zastavkin
36bl, Zsolt/Biczó 15tl; Wikipedia: 32br; World Bank Photo Collection 26b.

Every attempt has been made to clear copyright. Should there be any inadvertent
omission please apply to the publisher for rectification.

CONTENTS

IN THE HEADLINES

Banks often make the headlines, especially when a country is either making or losing a lot of money. In this book we take a look at the banking industry and find out how banks make big money, where the money goes, why banks matter and what the future holds for the industry.

Every day around the world, trillions of coins and paper money are exchanged.

The money you withdraw from cash machines has already passed through several banks.

Money, money, money

Every time we pay for shopping, order goods online or are paid for work, money is involved. Money pays for our food, clothes, hospitals, homes and transport. The bank acts as the middleman between the buyer and the seller, with the bank controlling the exchange of money.

A WORLD VIEW

Banking is a global industry. There are thousands of banks around the world making sure that money can pass from person to person, business to business and country to country. The banking industry enables money to flow around the world.

CHAPTER 1
ALL ABOUT BANKS

Banks trade in money and make a lot of money in the process, but what exactly is money? For most people, money is the metal coins and paper money in their purse or wallet that they exchange for goods and services. Money has an agreed value, or worth, so it can be used to buy things.

Different types of money

Money is a type of currency, something that has an agreed value. Anything can be used as money, as long as everyone agrees on the value of the items being used. Often the value is linked to how difficult the items are to obtain.

In China, cowrie shells, from islands in the Indian Ocean, were used as an early form of money. The shells were light and easy to carry.

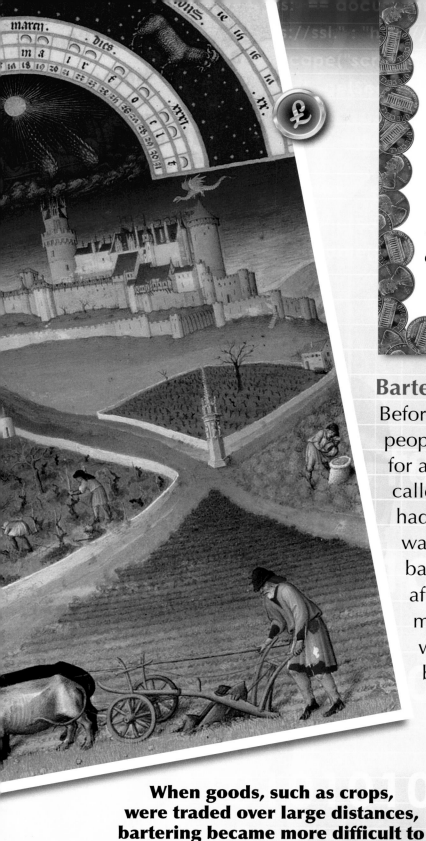

CURRENCY EXCHANGE

If you go abroad, you will first need to buy some of the other country's currency so that you have money to spend when you get there. A bank will exchange your pounds for paper money or coins in the foreign currency.

Bartering leads to money

Before money was invented, people swapped one thing for another in an exchange called bartering. If a farmer had a lot of barley but wanted a cow, he could barter his barley for a cow, after first agreeing how much barley the cow was worth. If he ran out of barley but needed wheat, he could swap his cow for an agreed amount of wheat. A simpler way of doing business was to use money, which represented an agreed value.

When goods, such as crops, were traded over large distances, bartering became more difficult to manage and money was invented.

BANKING'S ANCIENT ROOTS

Banks lend money. This tradition can be traced back to the eighteenth century BCE, when priests in Babylon lent money to merchants. In ancient Greece banking activities became more varied. Loans and deposits were made, currencies exchanged and coins weighed to check their value was correct.

The first banks

During the Middle Ages merchants wanted money for their goods, and many rich people, called nobles, needed loans to buy goods from the merchants. The earliest banks were places where merchants could store their money and nobles could obtain loans.

One of the oldest surviving banks is the Monte dei Paschi (originally Monte Pio) founded in Siena, Italy, in 1472.

THE GOLD STANDARD

The gold standard is a system in which the value of a country's currency is directly linked to gold. You used to be able to go into a bank in the United Kingdom and swap pounds for its value in gold. The country stopped using the gold standard in 1931.

Today, many central banks still keep stores of gold.

Early paper money

During the English Civil War (1642–1651) people often hid their money and jewels in the vault of the local goldsmith, who kept their valuables safe for a fee. The goldsmiths gave the owners a receipt, which they used to withdraw their valuables whenever they wanted. In time, the receipts were used as evidence that a person had enough money to pay for something. Like early paper money, the receipts were used as promises of money.

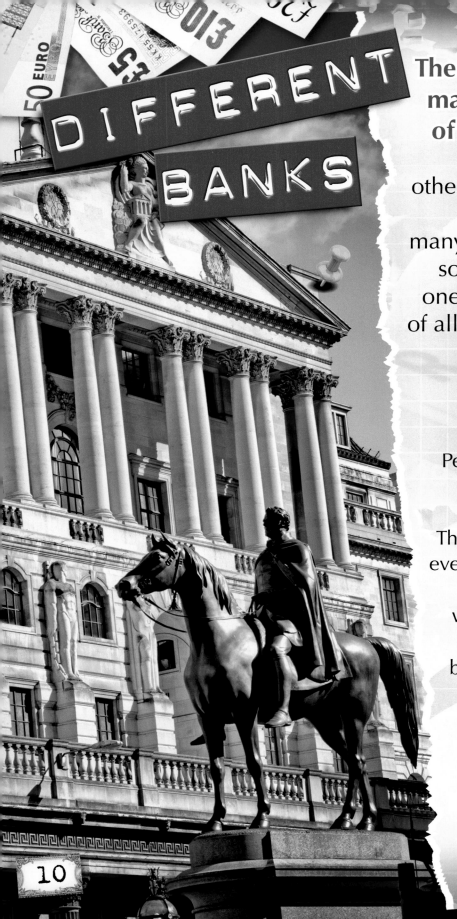

DIFFERENT BANKS

The banking industry is made up of thousands of banks. Some operate independently, while others are owned by larger banks. Each bank has many branches (buildings), sometimes in more than one country. The business of all banks, whatever their size or type, is money and making a profit.

Banks for everyone

People use banks for taking out money and putting it into their bank accounts. These banks can be used by everyone. Private banks look after the finances of very wealthy people and invest their money. Investment banks work for companies and invest their money to make more money.

The Bank of England is responsible for making sure that the British government does not run out of money.

The country's money

Most countries have a central bank that looks after the government's money. For example, in the United Kingdom the central bank is the Bank of England, in Australia it is the Reserve Bank of Australia and in New Zealand it is the Reserve Bank of New Zealand.

For some people, visiting a bank manager is still preferable to banking online. The bank manager can answer any questions and offer advice.

FUTURE FACT

Online banking can be done 24/7 as long as you have an Internet connection. It is cheaper for banks because they do not need to pay for as many staff or rent as many buildings. Many more people are likely to bank online in the future.

WHO RUNS THE BANKS?

The chief executive is the top boss responsible for running a bank. If the bank has many divisions or branches, these are run by branch managers.

Sharing the profit

Many banks are partly owned by a large number of people, called shareholders, who own a tiny part, or share, of the bank. The shareholders have some say in how the bank is run, depending on how many shares they own. When the bank makes a profit, the shareholders are given a portion of the profit.

The return shareholders receive for their investment in a bank depends on how well the bank invests its money.

The Prudential Regulation Authority (PRA) is part of the Bank of England. It checks that British banks, such as RBS, are operating safely and fairly.

What is a co-operative bank?

A co-operative bank is owned and run by its customers. It concentrates on meeting the needs of its customers, rather than just on making a profit.

PROTECTING SAVERS

Each country has its own rules and regulations for banks to follow. In the United Kingdom, if banks protected by the Financial Services Compensation Scheme (FSCS) go bust (run out of money), the FSCS promises to give back savers their money (up to a limit of £85,000). In Australia, the Financial Claims Scheme (FCS) is a similar arrangement.

CHAPTER 2

THE BUSINESS OF BANKS

It is safer to keep large sums of money in a bank rather than in a cupboard at home, so people put their savings in a bank account. An account is a personal record of how much money you have in the bank. It details how much you deposit and withdraw, and when you do this.

Making money

Banks must make money so they can pay their expenses and make a profit. To make money, they must do something with the money you deposit. What the bank does is either lend your money to other people or invest the money.

Banks lend money to businesspeople, who invest the money in their business.

14

Banks earn interest on the money that you give them.

Interest

Banks reward you for letting them look after your savings by paying you. The money they pay you is called interest. The amount they pay is a percentage of your savings, at a set rate. For example, if you save £60 in a bank for a year and the interest rate is 5 per cent, you will gain £3 (5 per cent of 60) at the end of the year, giving you £63. Banks can afford to pay interest because they make a big profit on the money that you save with them.

A SAFE RESERVE

Banks need to be able to pay money out to their savers whenever they want it, so they keep a reserve of cash. In the past, some banks lent more money than they had in the reserve and some people lost their savings. Today, new rules say that banks must keep more money in the bank.

DEBT PAYS

The more money a bank lends, the more money it makes. This is because most banks do not lend money for free!

Expensive loans

Homes, cars and holidays are expensive things to buy. People often borrow the money they need to pay for them from a bank. The bank makes money from these loans by charging interest, and the borrower pays back more money than they needed to borrow in the first place. When a person borrows money, he or she is in debt. Banks make profit when a person or company is in debt to the bank.

Interest-free

Islamic banking, which follows Sharia (Islamic) law, does not allow payment of interest. Instead, the bank and customer share any risk or profit from investments made.

The banking system of Islamic countries, such as Pakistan, is entirely different from countries in the West.

Banks make huge amounts of money from mortgages, which are large loans that people take out to help them buy homes.

STATE BANK OF PAKISTAN

50

FIFTY RUPE

COUNTRIES IN DEBT

Banks lend money to governments. Sometimes the amount a country owes in interest payments adds up to more than the original debt. Zimbabwe owes 150 per cent of the amount of money that the country makes (its Gross Domestic Product), Japan owes 227 per cent, the United Kingdom owes 90 per cent and Australia owes just 20 per cent.

17

INVESTING MONEY

Trading shares

Investment bankers buy and sell shares for companies and wealthy individuals. If a company does well, the value of the shares goes up. If it does not do well, the shares are worth less. Anyone who buys shares when the price is low and sells them when it is high, makes a profit.

Banks can make money by investing it. This means they buy shares in large companies or organisations that they believe will be successful. If the investment does well, the bank will make a profit.

Buying shares in property-development companies can make money for banks.

Investment bankers make or lose money, depending on the success of their investments.

Risking it all

Some organisations are prepared to buy shares in risky projects if there is a chance they might make a big profit. Often, the higher the risk, the greater the profit. This makes the investment banker's job exciting, but also more stressful.

SUDDEN LOSS

Unexpected disasters, such as the BP oil spill in the Gulf of Mexico in 2010, can cause a company to lose billions of pounds. If that happens, its share price may fall. Any bank owning shares in the company would not make much profit if it sold its shares at the time of the disaster.

A PROFITABLE INDUSTRY

Banks make most of their money by charging a high interest on loans and paying a lower interest on savings. The difference between the two amounts is the bank's profit. They also make money by charging for their services.

People must pay for the services banks offer, such as expensive credit cards.

FUTURE FACT

Banks take a risk when they lend someone money because there is no guarantee that the person will be able to pay it all back. If the bank thinks someone may not be able to pay it all back, they often charge a higher interest rate.

Different charges

Banks charge employers a fee for putting an employee's wages directly into their bank account. They may also charge people a fee when they pay bills from their account or make purchases.

Pensions benefit the banks as well as retired people.

Pension funds

Banks also make money from pension funds.
A person puts regular amounts into a pension fund and the bank invests the money by buying and selling stocks and shares. When the person retires, the bank gives them their pension money, with added interest, based on the success of the investments. The bank keeps the extra profit from pension money investment.

COSTS

Banks have a lot of costs. One major cost is the tax they have to pay to the government. The amount varies from country to country, but it can be as much as one-quarter of the bank's overall profit.

Profit and loss

Banks must pay for staff, office costs and technology. Despite these overheads, banks usually make good profits. However, if a bank is not in profit, it may sell off parts of its business. HSBC sold the US section of its credit card business to a credit card company for a profit of £1.43 billion. New owner Capital One took on £17.66 billion of customer loans.

The Bank of China has branches all over the world. The running costs of large banks such as this are enormous.

Financial organisations sponsor many sporting events.

Sponsoring events

From major sporting events to exhibitions and arts performances, banks often sponsor popular events. They do this for publicity and to encourage new customers. The bank often manages the finances of the event and this brings in more money for the bank to invest.

PRINTING COSTS

A country's central bank provides private banks with their money, but it costs central banks money to print money. For example, the US government produced 6.4 billion new bills in 2009. Each one cost 9.6 cents to make. This was nearly twice the cost of making a dollar bill in 2008. The rise was due to the increase in the cost of cotton (three-quarters of a dollar bill is made from cotton).

MAKING A PROFIT

In 2013, the US bank Wells Fargo became the world's most profitable bank, with a profit of $21.9 billion. In the same year, Barclays, HSBC, Lloyds Banking Group and RBS made a combined profit of £16.5 billion in the first half of 2013. Where does profit like that go?

Many people believe that bankers should no longer receive enormous bonuses.

BONUS BILLIONS

In 2014, bankers at RBS received the news that they would not receive the huge bonuses that the bank had planned to give them. RBS was told by the Treasury that it would not be allowed to pay its bankers bonuses twice the size of their salaries until the bank had recovered from the financial crisis of 2008.

Top bankers earn millions of dollars and enjoy luxurious lifestyles.

Bonuses big and small

The people who work for a bank as tellers or in administration sometimes receive a small bonus if the bank makes a good profit. The bankers (the people who set up the deals that earn huge profits) often receive enormous bonuses.

Good thing or bad?

Many people argue that bankers' bonuses are too high, especially when a country is in recession and many people are out of work. The banks argue that they need to pay bonuses to keep the most successful bankers from working elsewhere.

CHAPTER 4
THE BANKING WORLD

There is one bank that you cannot open an account with or borrow money from, unless you are a country! The World Bank is made up of 187 member countries. It gets its money from interest made on its investments and from fees paid by its members. The bank's aim is to encourage strong economies and reduce world poverty.

How it started

The World Bank was first set up in 1944, when it was called the International Bank for Reconstruction and Development (IBRD). It was set up to help economies recover after the devastating effects of the Second World War (1939–45).

The World Bank is made up of bankers from countries all over the world.

IF YOU ARE POOR

The World Bank puts money into projects in developing countries.

Role of the World Bank

The World Bank lends money to countries at either a low level of interest or no interest at all. This means the countries do not end up having to pay back a lot of extra money. Every year, the World Bank lends or gives grants worth almost £18 billion. Much of the money is spent on projects such as building highways and dams, or supplying clean, fresh drinking water.

CENTRAL BANK

Every day a country's banks have to deposit a certain amount of money in the country's central bank. Central banks lend money to banks when no one else will. This is called 'acting as the lender of last resort'.

27

INFLATION

One hundred years ago, you could buy much more with one pound than you can today. The same pound was worth more. This is due to inflation. Inflation is the rise in the general cost of living, such as the price of clothes, food and gas. As inflation rises, a pound will buy you less because prices are higher.

Some people argue that printing more money causes inflation. More available money means there is more money than goods to buy. This pushes up prices.

Shops often offer huge reductions to encourage people to spend.

Who sets the interest rate?

There are many things that influence inflation, including interest rates. A country's central bank usually sets the interest rate, which other banks follow quite closely. In general, if the interest rate is high, people spend less because they are paying more interest on their debts.

RISING COSTS

In 2008, the rate of inflation in Zimbabwe reached a staggering 231 million per cent! Prices in shops doubled almost every other day. When there is a crisis such as this, a bank's product (money) is no longer worth much. People can more usefully trade in bags of rice, apples or flour.

Low interest rates

Sometimes the bank sets low interest rates to encourage people to borrow money to pay for homes or goods. People are more likely to borrow if they do not have to make high interest payments. Low interest rates are good for borrowers but bad for savers. Savers make less money from the interest on their savings when interest rates are low.

THE BIG PLAYERS

There are thousands of different banks around the world. HSBC and Bank of America are two of the major players. The information following shows the huge figures involved in running a big bank.

World presence

In 2014, HSBC had:
- 60 million customers, including both businesses and individuals.
- A net worth of £1.59 trillion.
- 254,066 employees worldwide.
- Offices in more than 80 countries around the world. Its offices can be found in Asia, North America, South America, Europe and Africa.

After much public protest, Bank of America cancelled its monthly charge of $5.00 for customers to use their bank cards.

What do banks buy?

Bank of America bought:
- MBNA, a leading issuer of credit cards, in 2005.
- The mortgage lender Countrywide Financial in June 2008.
- Investment bank Merrill Lynch for $50 billion in 2008.

The US government gave Bank of America $45 billion to help pay off the huge debts that the bank inherited when it bought Merrill Lynch. Bank of America has now repaid this money.

The Marine Midland building in New York houses HSBC's US offices.

BIGGEST BANKS

The Industrial and Commercial Bank of China (ICBC) is one of the world's most profitable banks. In 2011, it made a net profit of $32.5 billion and was declared the most profitable bank in the world in that year.

CHAPTER 5

WHAT CAN GO WRONG?

Banks are meant to keep money safe and help people save. Sometimes, however, things go very wrong. If a bank puts too much money into a particular type of loan or investment, it may lose so much money that it is forced to close down. Another reason a bank may fail is if people cannot pay back their loans.

A domino effect

If one bank suffers, it is likely the trouble will spread to other banks. This happens because banks make loans to each other. If one bank makes a loss and fails, the other banks that lent money to the failed bank will not get their money back, so they end up in trouble, too.

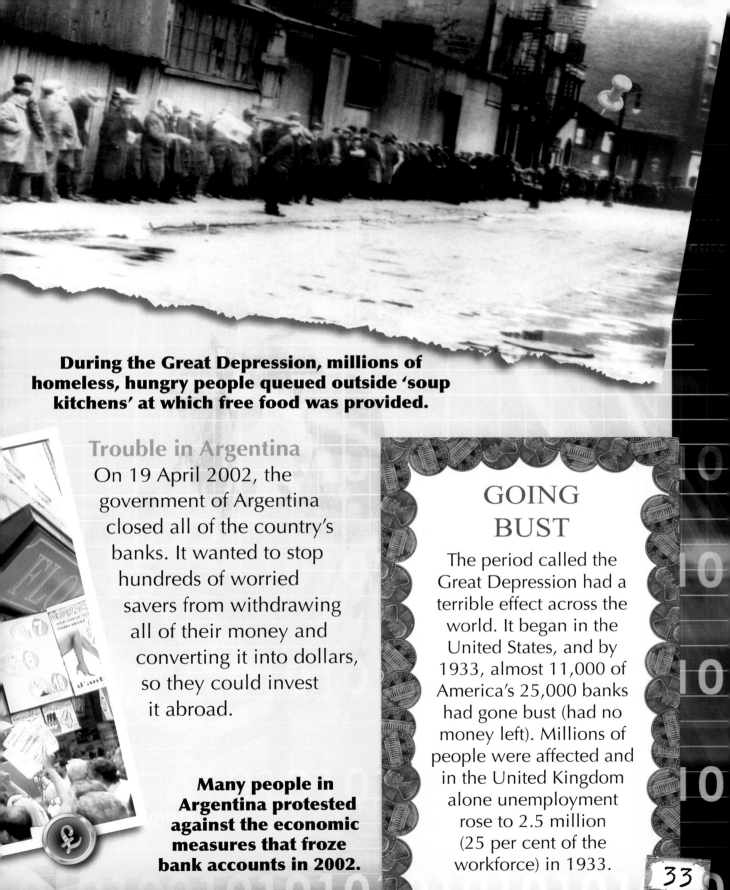

During the Great Depression, millions of homeless, hungry people queued outside 'soup kitchens' at which free food was provided.

Trouble in Argentina

On 19 April 2002, the government of Argentina closed all of the country's banks. It wanted to stop hundreds of worried savers from withdrawing all of their money and converting it into dollars, so they could invest it abroad.

Many people in Argentina protested against the economic measures that froze bank accounts in 2002.

GOING BUST

The period called the Great Depression had a terrible effect across the world. It began in the United States, and by 1933, almost 11,000 of America's 25,000 banks had gone bust (had no money left). Millions of people were affected and in the United Kingdom alone unemployment rose to 2.5 million (25 per cent of the workforce) in 1933.

MELTDOWN

In 2007, an international banking crisis began in the United States. Overnight banks that had been successful went bankrupt. The domino effect spread around the world and caused a global economic disaster.

Rumours of crisis

Banks in the United States had been offering mortgages to huge numbers of people, including many who were unable to pay back the loans. As more and more people failed to make their monthly repayments, rumours of a crisis in the banking industry soon spread around the world.

Overnight, employees of Lehman Brothers lost their jobs and had to pack their things and leave.

34

During the banking crisis many people had to leave their homes, which were sold by the banks.

Collapse of Lehman Brothers

Lehman Brothers was the fourth-largest investment bank in the United States. It owned two companies that had sold mortgages without checking thoroughly that the borrowers could repay their monthly loans. The bank had also 'fiddled its books' to show that it had more money than it actually did. In 2008, Lehman Brothers had to stop operating because it had no more money. It had lent about £380 billion to people and businesses, and was only owed £368 billion.

FUTURE FACT

Many banks lost money during the 2008 banking crisis, so they were unable to lend as much. This meant people bought fewer things and many small businesses failed. The domino effect is still being felt today.

BANKING FRAUD

At the end of each day, bank tellers make sure all their sums add up. They must check that they have not given anyone too much money, and that they have accounted for all deposits that have been made. Small errors are one problem that the banking industry faces. A much bigger problem is deliberate fraud.

Special marks and lines on bills help prevent fraud.

Grand theft

Fraudsters are not film-style bank-robbers with guns and masks. Instead they use computers to steal billions from banks each year. Card fraud has reached enormous proportions in the United States. In 2012, more than $11 billion was stolen from US banks through both credit and debit card fraud. In the United Kingdom £450 million was stolen through credit card fraud in 2013.

Money can be stolen from people's bank accounts when they unknowingly give their account details over the phone to fraudulent companies and institutions.

FUTURE FACT

Many of the fees that banks charge go towards paying back money to victims of banking fraud. As more and more people bank online, banks will spend money on expensive systems to try to prevent fraud.

Rogue trader

Investment banks carry out checks so they know what their employees are doing, but sometimes the checks fail. In 1995, British trader Nick Leeson, working for Barings Bank Plc, lost the bank £827 million. Barings Bank collapsed and was sold to Dutch bank ING for just £1!

ECONOMIC RECOVERY

Today, during difficult times, governments do not just let the banking industry collapse. They help the banks out. Since 2007, this has happened the world over.

In 2007, the Bank of England gave failing Northern Rock an emergency loan to help it survive.

Government loans

When the banking system is in serious trouble, governments can lend or give the banks money to help them recover. In 2008, the British government put £37 billion into the banking industry by buying shares in some of the banks. This stopped the banks from failing. The banks have now paid back a lot of this money.

In 2008, former British prime minister Gordon Brown pledged to revive the British economy.

New rules

Since the banking industry's crisis in 2008, new rules have been set for banks to follow. These rules, known as the Basel Accord, were agreed by a group of men and women from many of the central banks and financial authorities. Recent Basel Accord rules state that banks must keep more money in reserve to deal with any losses they make. It is up to each country to follow the rules.

CHAPTER 6

BANKING IN THE FUTURE

Banking on a smartphone is especially convenient because it can be done anywhere.

Banking in the future will be very different from traditional banking. Technology is changing our world all the time, and the banking industry is embracing the changes. More and more people are using online banking, which they can turn to 24/7. Using smartphone apps, they can even bank on the move.

Canada issued $100 plastic notes in 2011, and released $50 bills in 2012.

Plastic money

Money made from a type of plastic was first issued as currency in Australia in 1988. The plastic money lasts for longer than paper money and is less easy to forge. Now countries from Romania to Papua New Guinea use plastic, too.

Cashless country

The Central Bank of Nigeria plans to go virtually cashless, with e-payments replacing cash in many transactions. Many Nigerians do not use banks, however, because they live too far from towns. It remains to be seen how people without bank accounts or access to cash machines will fit into the cashless society.

FUTURE FACT

Today, some banks have no bank teller, just touch screens. Some bank cards use fingerprint recognition instead of a signature. People are beginning to question whether traditional banks have a place in the future.

BETTER BANKING?

When you save with a bank, you do not know where the bank will invest your money. It could be loaned to companies that supply arms to bad regimes, or to multinational companies that do not care if they damage the environment.

Investing with care

Ethical banks invest only in companies that they believe will benefit society or the environment. They may put money into green projects, for example, or into companies that work to help young people. They still aim to make a profit, but they choose where to invest carefully.

Ethical banks invest in projects that encourage the fair treatment of workers, such as tea plantation workers.

Around the world, people have been protesting about the influence of banks on the economic crisis.

Making a stand

Since the global economic crisis of 2008, people have been protesting about how wrong it seems that the banks continue to make huge profits while so many ordinary people have lost their jobs and suffered financial hardship. They argue that it was the banks that caused the financial crisis in the first place. The international protest movement Occupy wants banking to be less about profit and more about responsibility.

FUTURE FACT

Some banks have started to lend small sums to poor people in developing countries so they can start up businesses, even though small loans are expensive to manage. The banks are beginning to see how much small loans can improve lives in the future.

BANK ON IT

The global financial crisis that started in 2008 has made people realise just how dependent they all are on the banking industry. People want to be sure that the banks cannot cause a similar crisis in the future.

Greece in trouble

Greece owes banks in other countries many billions. It borrowed much of the money from banks in other European countries. Central banks are still trying to work out how to manage this banking crisis.

44

The European Central Bank has provided money to failing European economies to try to prevent them collapsing.

Containing the damage

As we have already seen, a major disaster in one bank or one country can have a serious domino effect around the world. New rules will help to contain the massive industry and lessen the risk of such crises.

Banking is changing with supermarkets such as Tesco now offering banking services.

FUTURE FACT

Non-banking businesses are beginning to recognise the profits to be made from offering banking services. Tesco stores, for example, are trying to attract customers by offering some cheaper banking services.

GLOSSARY

bank a financial organisation that lets you put in and withdraw money

bank account a record of how much money you have in a bank, how much you put in and withdraw and when you make the transactions

bankrupt when a business or bank runs out of money and can no longer offer its services

bank tellers people working at bank counters

bartering a system of exchange, swapping goods and services

bonus extra money on top of a person's wage

central bank a bank that looks after a government's money

currency something people use to buy and sell goods and services

debt what an individual or company owes

deposit put into a bank

economy the flow of money in a country and how much money the country makes through businesses

exchange swap

finances to do with money

forge copy illegally

inflation a rise in a lot of prices at the same time

interest the amount of money (shown as a percentage) that can be earned or charged for saving or borrowing money

investment to spend money in the hope of making a profit

loan a thing that has been borrowed, such as a sum of money. Usually the lender expects the borrower to return the loan at a later date.

merchants people involved in trade, often to another country

mortgages large loans to buy homes

pensions monies that people save up to live on when they stop working

percentage a way of showing how large or small an amount is compared to another. The mathematical symbol is %.

profit money that a business makes on top of the money it has spent or invested

purchases goods a person has bought

rate the amount of interest charged

share a small part of a company that a person can buy. Companies sell shares to raise money.

shareholders people who own shares

sponsor to give money towards something, usually in return for publicity

stocks the money that a corporation raises through the sale of shares, or the number of shares that somebody owns

tax money that is paid to the government

trader someone who buys and sells

withdraw take out

FOR MORE INFORMATION

BOOKS

Banks and Banking (World Economy Explained),
Sean Connolly, Franklin Watts

Show Me the Money, Alvin D. Hall, DK

*Money Doesn't Grow on Trees: A Guide to Managing
Your Money*, Paul Mason, Wayland

WEBSITES

Find out more about the banking industry at:

www.sciencekids.co.nz/sciencefacts/technology/money.html

www.fdic.gov/about/learn/learning/index.html

www.hrp.org.uk/TowerOfLondon/stories/palacehighlights/CoinsandKings/
mintmaster

Note to parents and teachers
Every effort has been made by the Publisher to ensure that these websites contain no inappropriate or offensive
material. However, because of the nature of the Internet, it is impossible to guarantee that the contents of these
sites will not be altered. We strongly advise that Internet access is supervised by a responsible adult.

INDEX